Disney

HIGH SCHOOL MUSICAL
THE CONCERT

ALONG FOR THE RIDE

Photos and Introduction by Marc Blackwell

Based on the Disney Channel Original Movie
"High School Musical," Written by Peter Barsocchini

DISNEY PRESS
New York

DISNEY CHANNEL

THAT'S ME!

IN NOVEMBER OF 2006, MY BEST FRIEND,

LUCAS GRABEEL (AKA RYAN EVANS), INVITED ME "ALONG FOR THE RIDE"

TO TAKE PICTURES AS HE AND THE CAST OF HIGH SCHOOL MUSICAL—THE CONCERT

TRAVELED FROM CITY TO CITY ACROSS NORTH AMERICA PUTTING ON A ROCKIN'

CONCERT EVERY NIGHT FOR TWO MONTHS. WE TRAVELED IN BIG TOUR BUSES THAT

WOULD TAKE US FROM ARENA TO ARENA. IN EACH CITY LUCAS (RYAN), ASHLEY

TISDALE (SHARPAY), CORBIN BLEU (CHAD), VANESSA HUDGENS (GABRIELLA),

MONIQUE COLEMAN (TAYLOR), AND DREW SEELEY (TROY) WOULD PUT ON THE

AMAZING NINETY-MINUTE SHOW. AFTER WRAPPING UP THE FORTY-THREE CITY U.S.

TOUR, WE PACKED UP THE SHOW AND WENT TO SOUTH AMERICA AND DID TEN MORE

SHOWS! I WAS THERE THE ENTIRE TIME, SIDE BY SIDE WITH YOUR FAVORITE STARS,

TAKING PICTURES ONSTAGE, BEHIND THE CURTAINS, ON THE BUSES AND PLANES, IN

THE DRESSING ROOMS, AND EVERYWHERE ELSE IN BETWEEN. NOW THAT THE TOUR

IS OVER AND THE FILM HAS BEEN DEVELOPED, I AM INVITING YOU TO CLIMB ABOARD

JUST LIKE I DID. SO BUCKLE UP, HOLD ON TIGHT, AND ENJOY THE RIDE!

—MARC BLACKWELL

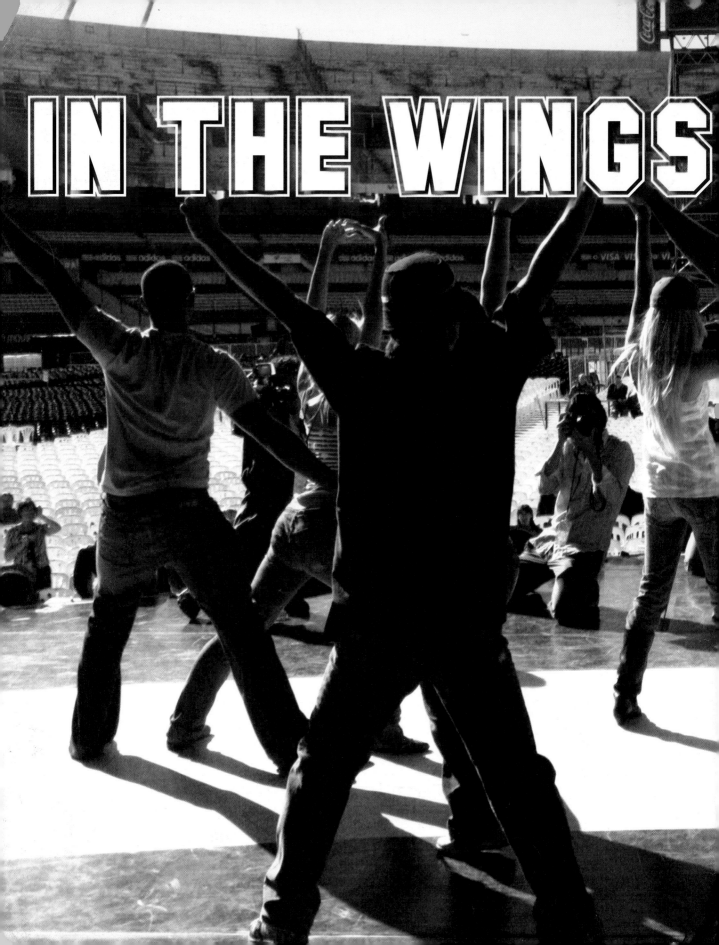

IN THE WINGS

THE CAST MEMBERS POLISH THEIR DANCE MOVES DURING REHEARSAL.

DO-RE-MI! VANESSA AND DREW WARM UP THEIR VOICES.

THE PERFORMERS GET THEIR
HEADS IN THE GAME . . .

. . . (AND GOOF OFF
A LITTLE BIT)!

THESE SINGERS REACH FOR THE RAFTERS WITH EVERY NOTE.

TA-DA! STRIKE A POSE.

MONIQUE SHOWS OFF HER DANCIN' MOVES.

LUCAS HITS A HIGH NOTE.

LUCAS

A RAINBOW OF BACKUP DANCERS GETS READY FOR "BOP TO THE TOP."

CORBIN JUMPS FOR THE STARS.

MONIQUE, DREW, LUCAS, AND ASHLEY PUT THEIR HEARTS AND SOULS INTO THEIR SINGING.

THE CAST CAN'T WAIT UNTIL THIS EMPTY ARENA FILLS UP WITH FANS!

PRACTICE MAKES PERFECT!

THE DANCERS STRUT THEIR STUFF.

CHILLIN' OUT BETWEEN SONGS.

¡QUE FABULOSO, LUCAS!

CORBIN PREPARES TO LEAP INTO THE AIR.

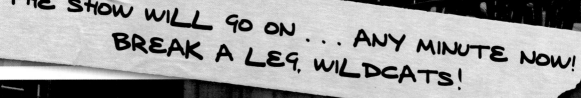

THE SHOW WILL GO ON . . . ANY MINUTE NOW! BREAK A LEG, WILDCATS!

ONSTAGE

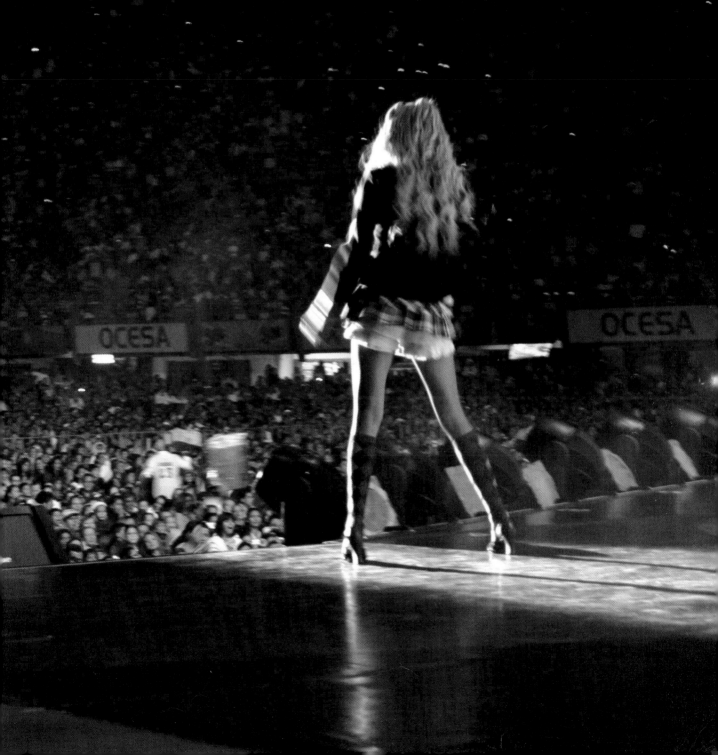

YOU GOTTA LOVE THOSE WILDCAT COLORS!

ALL THAT ENERGY LIGHTS UP THE STAGE!

THE EAST HIGH CREW PERFORMS "STICK TO THE STATUS QUO."

ASHLEY, CORBIN, VANESSA, DREW, MONIQUE, AND LUCAS SALUTE THE CROWD.

THOSE WILDCATS
SURE CAN DANCE!

CORBIN LEADS THE BAND IN A BRAND-NEW SCENE THAT WAS CREATED FOR THE TOUR.

VANESSA AND DREW
SING THEIR DUET.

VANESSA FLASHES A KILLER SMILE.

ONLY EAST HIGH STUDENTS WOULD SING IN THE CAFETERIA!

CHECK OUT THE TOUR'S LEADING MEN: DREW, CORBIN, AND LUCAS.

WHO DOESN'T LIKE A GOOD JAZZ SQUARE?

WE ❤ JAZZ SQUARES

LUCAS, ASHLEY, AND THE DANCERS END "BOP TO THE TOP" WITH A FLOURISH!

THE WILDCATS WAVE GOOD-BYE TO THEIR FANS.

THE ACTORS TAKE THEIR FINAL BOWS—TOGETHER, OF COURSE!

ON THE ROAD

ON THE ROAD AGAIN! LUCAS, DREW, AND ASHLEY TRAVEL TO THE NEXT SHOW BY BUS.

WHEN THE GANG VISITED A RANCH IN ARGENTINA, THEY HAD NO TROUBLE MAKING SOME FOUR-LEGGED FRIENDS.

FUN WITH FANS! THE CAST DID SEVERAL SIGNINGS DURING THE TOUR, AND THEY ALSO VISITED A CHILDREN'S HOSPITAL.

SAY CHEESE! THERE'S ALWAYS TIME TO SNAP SOME PHOTOS WITH FRIENDS ON THE ROAD.

DREW CHECKS OUT THE SIGNATURE WALL AT THE ROCK AND ROLL HALL OF FAME. (IS HE ABOUT TO ADD HIS NAME?)

GOTTA TAKE A PICTURE WITH THE MOUSE!

ROCK ON! THE CAST VISITS THE ROCK AND ROLL HALL OF FAME IN CLEVELAND. ARE WE LOOKING AT FUTURE INDUCTEES?

BACKSTAGE

PICTURE PERFECT: VANESSA GETS MADE UP BEFORE A SHOW.

ASHLEY ADDS ANOTHER COAT OF MASCARA.

THE GUYS MONKEY
AROUND BACKSTAGE.

SO MANY COSTUMES AND SO MANY HATS!

NO MIX-UPS, PLEASE! ALL OF VANESSA'S SOUND EQUIPMENT WAS LABELED IN YELLOW . . . .

...AND LUCAS'S IN ORANGE!

BRRRR, BRRRR, BRRRR, MAH! ASHLEY AND LUCAS WARM UP THEIR VOCAL CORDS.

THE CAST STRETCHES BEFORE GOING ONSTAGE.

HANGING OUT BACKSTAGE

THE CREW REALLY BECAME A PART OF THE FAMILY.

THE WILDCATS ARE A TEAM ONSTAGE AND OFF.

WAITING FOR THE SHOW TO START: LUCAS STRUMS HIS GUITAR, WHILE SOME CAST MEMBERS CATCH A FEW WINKS.

THE PRESHOW HUDDLE!

THE EAST HIGH CHAMPIONS WALK OFF STAGE VICTORIOUS.

GO WILDCATS!

TOUR 07

15 Y 16 De Mayo
Buenos Aires
Argentina

18 De Mayo
Santiago De Chile

22 De Mayo
Caracas Venezuela

24 Y 25 De Mayo
Monterrey, N. Leon-mexico
Auditorio Coca Cola

27 De Mayo
Ciudad De Mexico
Foro Sol

29 Y 30 De Mayo
Guadalajara - Mexico
Arena V.f.g. Jal.